P9-BBV-199

About the Author:

Dr. Daniela Owen is a psychologist in the SF Bay Area who brings to life healthy mind concepts and strategies for children everywhere. For more about the author please check out: drdanielaowen.com

For Lila Skye and Milo Grant

Copyright © 2020 by Puppy Dogs & Ice Cream, Inc.

All rights reserved. Published in the United States by Puppy Dogs & Ice Cream, Inc.

ISBN: 978-1-953177-02-5

Edition: June 2020

For all inquiries, please contact us at:

info@puppysmiles.org

To see more of our books, visit us at:

www.PuppyDogsAndIceCream.com

This book is given with love...

Sometimes, bad things happen in the world...

And they make us

feel scared.

Sometimes these things
make us worry about
what is going to happen next.

Our family, friends,
and neighbors
may all be affected.

All of this worry

can make us feel terrible…

Our tummies may seem

like they're tied up in knots.

It may feel hard to breathe,
like an elephant is
sitting on our chest.

Our heads may be so full
of worried thoughts
that we can't concentrate
on anything else.

But when this happens,
it is important
to remind ourselves
that we are fine, right now.

To help yourself calm down,
start by closing your eyes...

Then take 3 deep breaths...

breathe in slowly...

and breathe out slowly.

IN

OUT

IN

OUT

IN

OUT

Now, keep your eyes closed...
gently wrap your arms
around your body...
and give yourself a big, warm hug.

You can handle this,
because right now
you are here,
and you are not in any danger.

Let your body relax a little...
drop your shoulders...
and wiggle your toes.

You don't have to be
on high alert at this moment.

Let worrying thoughts
drift out of your mind.

The bad things
may still be happening...
but you don't have to worry
about them this minute.

Because right now,
you are fine.

What else can you do to relax?

Can you draw a pretty picture?

Can you look out the window
at the beautiful world outside?

Can you read a funny,

exciting, or adventurous book?

Can you play a fun game

or solve a tricky puzzle?

Can you cuddle a furry pet

or a favorite stuffed animal?

Then remind yourself...

Right now, I am fine.

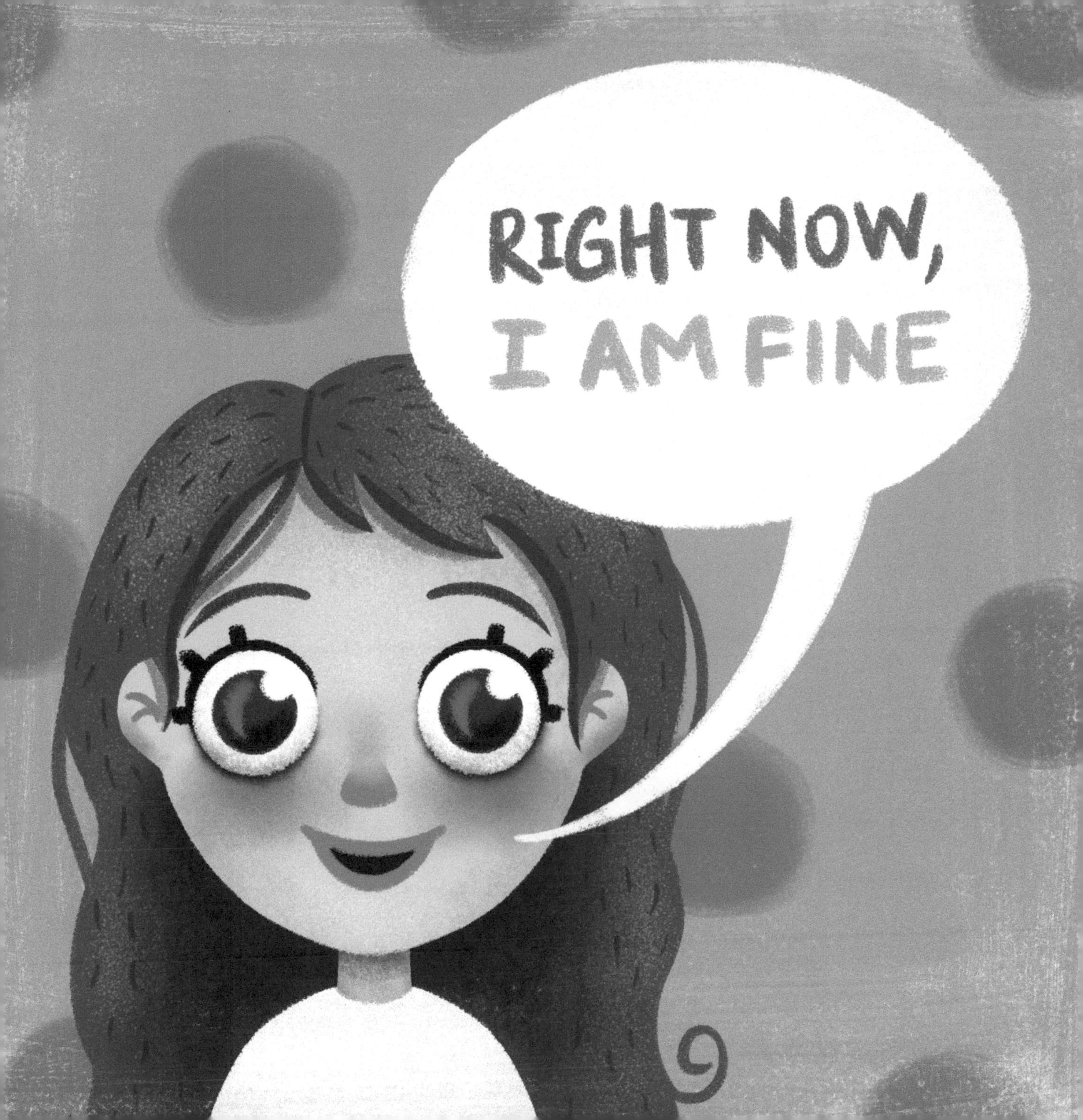
RIGHT NOW,
I AM FINE

CPSIA information can be obtained
at www.ICGtesting.com
Printed in the USA
LVHW011704070421
683705LV00004B/26